THE DEADLIEST SPIDER

Eleanor
Spicer Rice

illustrated by
Max Temescu

Norton Young Readers

An Imprint of W. W. Norton & Company
Independent Publishers Since 1923

Courtesy of

For more information visit
newkidsonthebooks.org

For Forrest, Gray, and Taco,
who never smash all the spiders. —E.S.R.
For Mom —M.T.

Text copyright © 2025 by Eleanor Spicer Rice
Illustrations copyright © 2025 by Max Temescu

For information about permission to reproduce selections from this book, write to
Permissions, W. W. Norton & Company, Inc., 500 Fifth Avenue, New York, NY 10110

For information about special discounts for bulk purchases, please contact
W. W. Norton Special Sales at specialsales@wwnorton.com or 800-233-4830

Manufacturing by Marquis
Book design by Hana Anouk Nakamura
Production manager: Delaney Adams

ISBN 978-1-324-05371-2 (cl)
978-1-324-08237-8 (pbk)

W. W. Norton & Company, Inc., 500 Fifth Avenue, New York, NY 10110
www.wwnorton.com

W. W. Norton & Company Ltd., 15 Carlisle Street, London W1D 3BS

1 2 3 4 5 6 7 8 9 0

WARNING!

YOU ARE ABOUT TO MEET THE DEADLIEST SPIDERS ON EARTH.

SOME MAY LIVE FAR AWAY. OTHERS MIGHT BE SLEEPING IN YOUR BEDROOM RIGHT NOW.

Two good rules for all spiders, deadly or not:

1. Do not touch! That means no grabbing, poking, stomping, tickling, kicking, or otherwise bothering them. What did they ever do to you?

2. Do not fear! That's right. Deadly or not, spiders fascinate. They're helpful and most are shy. Keep your distance. Pay attention. You might make some new friends.

In these pages, you will meet six types of spiders that we humans think are deadly. They all have powerful venom. Only one can be crowned THE DEADLIEST.

WHO WILL IT BE? THE SNEAKY BLACK WIDOW? THE AGGRESSIVE WANDERING SPIDER? OR SOMEONE ELSE? LET'S FIND OUT!

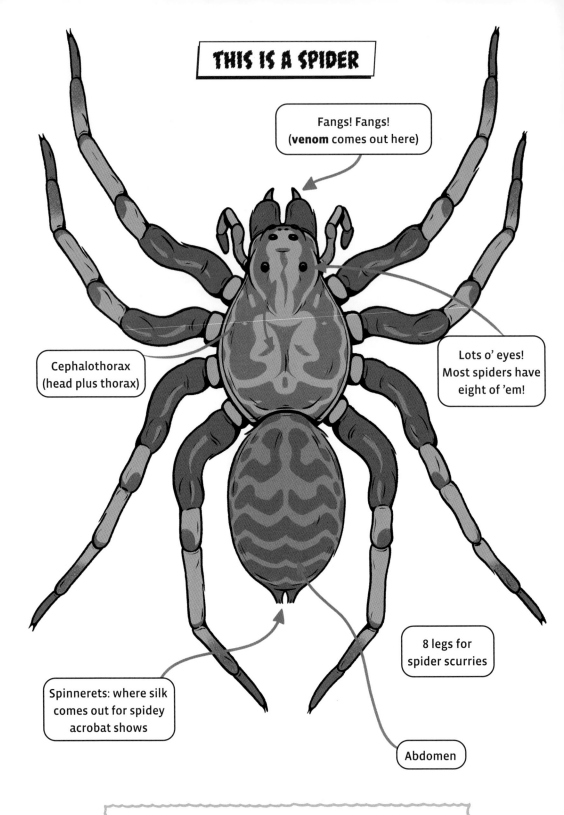

SPIDERS ARE NOT INSECTS

They belong to a group of animals called **arachnids** (uh-rak-nuhds).

Here are some arachnids that are not spiders:

Scorpions (pincers, and venom comes from the stinging tail instead of fangs)

Ticks (no fangs, six legs as babies)

Mites (no fangs, six legs as babies)

Daddy longlegs
(no fangs, no venom)

Peace out, other arachnids! This book is for fang fans only!

BUST THAT MYTH!

Daddy longlegs are not only nonvenomous; they're not spiders at all!

WHY DO WE THINK SPIDERS ARE DEADLY?

Nearly all spiders are **predators**. They use venom to calm or kill their prey. They also use it for defense.

> Ummm, how about a salad?

PREDATOR: an animal that eats other animals.

We fear spiders because some have powerful venom that could hurt or kill us.

Scientists believe these spiders evolved extra potent venom to help them calm their prey.

No, not humans. Humans are way too big for spiders to eat.

Besides, many spider species' fangs are tiny, too weak to puncture our skin.

In fact, fewer than 0.5% of spider species can hurt us at all.

> Wow! No, thank you!

Check out this hackled orb weaver, the only spider we know of that doesn't have venom. It uses a silken net to capture its prey.

THEY PRETTY MUCH ALL HAVE VENOM?! WHY DON'T WE JUST SMASH THEM ALL?

THREE REASONS YOU SHOULDN'T SMASH SPIDERS:

1. Spiders keep our **environment** healthy. They eat pests in our farms, forests, and homes.

They are also meals for all kinds of creatures, like birds and lizards.

ENVIRONMENT: the world in which plants and creatures live.

ARACHNOLOGIST: someone who studies spiders.

2. Arachnologists estimate that you are never more than four feet from a spider. Smashing them would be a full-time job. You have better things to do than smash spiders!

3. Spiders aren't all that scary. They're cool. Some dance and sing! They come in all shapes and sizes! Watch them! You will never be bored when a spider's around. And they're always around!

WE HAVE THEM! WE NEED THEM! LET'S LOVE THEM!

MEET THE CONTESTANTS

She has that hourglass on her abdomen and a pile of ex-husbands!
THE BLACK WIDOW!

Oh, don't be shy! Let's give a warm welcome to the **BROWN RECLUSE!**

Is it sand? Is it a mouthful of deadly? Meet the **SIX-EYED SAND SPIDER** —if you can find him!

WIDOW SPIDER

Number of people bitten each year: *thousands*
Distribution: *every continent except Antarctica*

Our first contestant is actually a group of closely related spiders called widows.

Ever heard of black widows? They're one species of widows that live in North America. Widows come in many colors and live all over the world.

Southern black widow
(North America)

White widow
(North Africa, the Middle East, and parts of Asia)

Red widow
(United States)

South American black widow
(South America)

Australian black widow (Australia,
New Zealand, and southeast Asia)

Brown widow
(worldwide)

Katipō
(New Zealand)

Why are they "widows"? Widows get their name from a myth that female widows eat their mates. The truth is, while many spider females eat their mates, black widows rarely do.

Phinda button spider
(South Africa)

I was framed!

WHAT HAPPENS IF A WIDOW BITES YOU?

Widow females have large venom glands. Their bites can be dangerous. Widow venom contains a **neurotoxin** called latrotoxin. Latrotoxin causes a condition called latrodectism.

First, your muscles will hurt. Bad.

You could start sweating like you've just run a marathon.

Your belly could cramp. Your muscles will begin to spasm.

Your heart will race.

NEUROTOXIN: a poison that affects the nerves.

Latrodectism could last a few days or several weeks.

But widows don't like to bite and will only do so if they feel their lives are in immediate danger. Try to never put a black widow's life in immediate danger! Stay away!

DO NOT challenge it to a dance-off with your spidey fingers!

DO NOT try to give it a kiss!

COOL FACT:

Black widow silk is so strong that in World Wars I and II people used it to make the crosshairs of gun sights. People harvested silk from black widow spiders in factories.

DO NOT try to put it between two slices of toast to make a widow sandwich!

LATRODECTISM SOUNDS HARSH. BUT IS IT AS BAD AS THE WHAMMY PACKED BY THE BROWN RECLUSE? LET'S FIND OUT!

RECLUSE SPIDER

Number of people bitten each year: *thousands*
Distribution: *every continent except Antarctica*

Arizona brown spider
(United States)

Brown recluse
(North America)

Many of us have heard of the brown recluse, found in parts of the United States and Mexico.

Like widows, recluse spiders are actually a group of different species found around the world.

Namibian recluse
(Southern Africa)

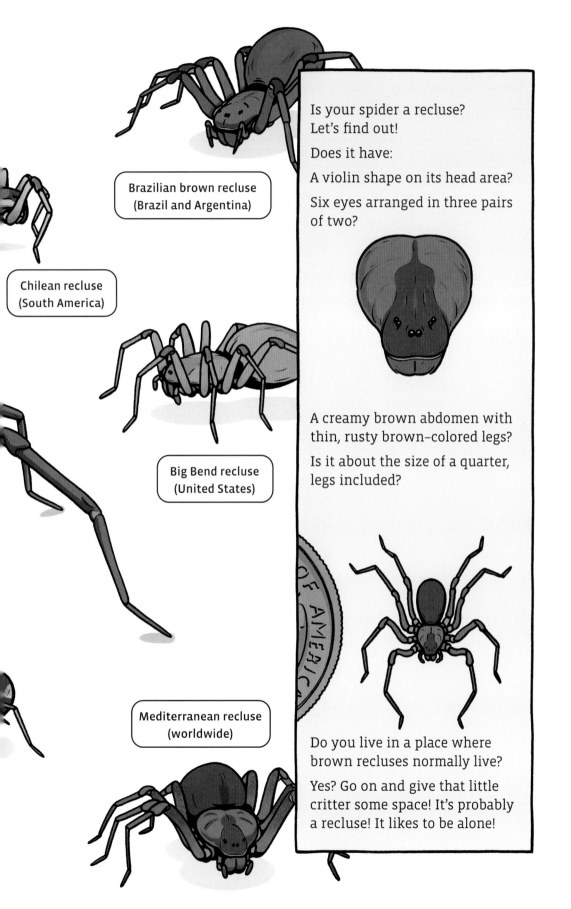

Brazilian brown recluse
(Brazil and Argentina)

Chilean recluse
(South America)

Big Bend recluse
(United States)

Mediterranean recluse
(worldwide)

Is your spider a recluse?
Let's find out!

Does it have:

A violin shape on its head area?

Six eyes arranged in three pairs of two?

A creamy brown abdomen with thin, rusty brown–colored legs?

Is it about the size of a quarter, legs included?

Do you live in a place where brown recluses normally live?

Yes? Go on and give that little critter some space! It's probably a recluse! It likes to be alone!

WHAT HAPPENS IF A RECLUSE BITES YOU?

Recluse venom has:

Toxin

Toxin spreaders to help it move quickly through your body

Allergic response triggers

Insect nervous system attackers

Blood disrupters: One disrupts clots. One disrupts blood pressure.

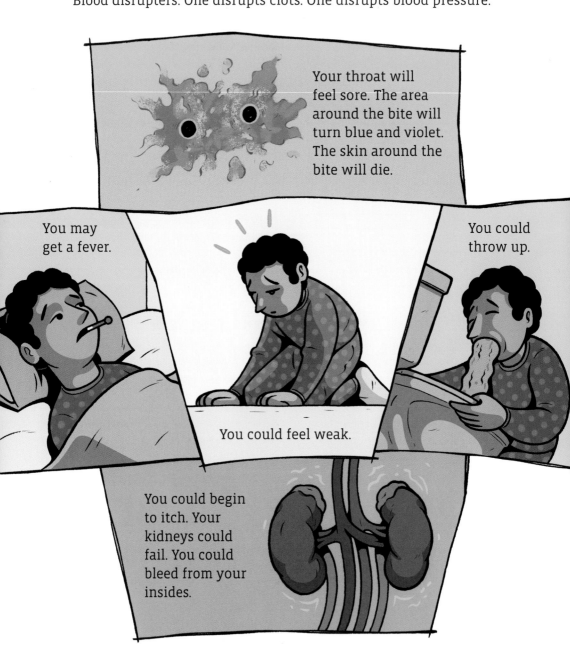

Your throat will feel sore. The area around the bite will turn blue and violet. The skin around the bite will die.

You may get a fever.

You could throw up.

You could feel weak.

You could begin to itch. Your kidneys could fail. You could bleed from your insides.

Those of us who live with recluse spiders are often surrounded by them.

Even so, they rarely hurt us.

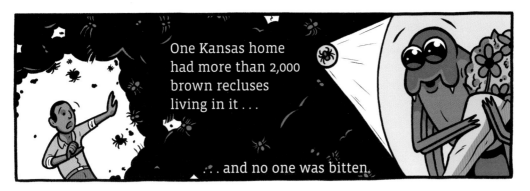

They spend about 90% of their time hanging out in their webs, hiding from you, and eating your household pests.

BROWN RECLUSES CAN HURT, BUT CAN THEY BE THE DEADLIEST?

That's better.

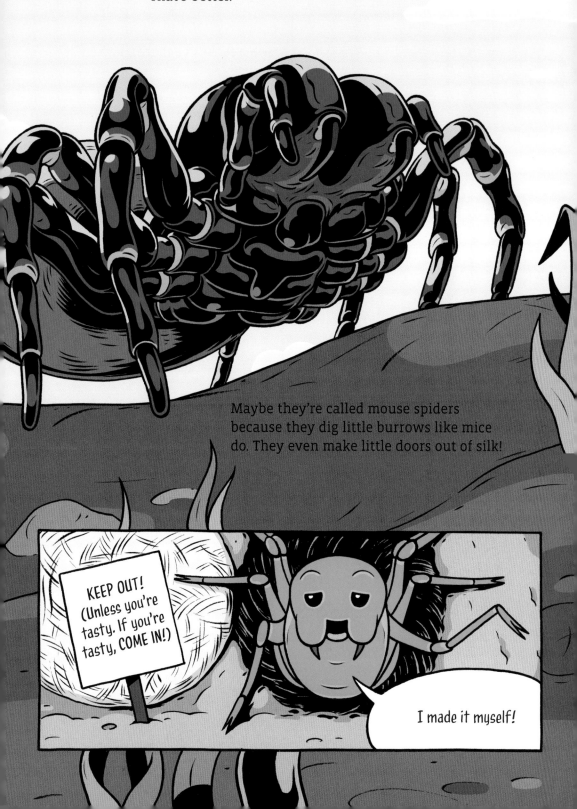

Maybe they're called mouse spiders because they dig little burrows like mice do. They even make little doors out of silk!

KEEP OUT! (Unless you're tasty. If you're tasty, COME IN!)

I made it myself!

Or maybe it's because they could eat mice if they wanted to (not as adorable).

Or maybe it's because they're big enough that people could mistake them for mice (OK, we'll stop now).

We're not sure why they're called mouse spiders, but these tarantula-like spiders have giant fangs.

Because they live in tunnels with trapdoors, mouse spiders are often mistaken for another feared Australian arachnid: the funnel-web spider.

WHAT HAPPENS IF A MOUSE SPIDER BITES YOU?

First, you would see a puncture wound from their giant fangs.

Mouse spiders can give dry bites. A dry bite is a bite that has no venom in it.

What if it isn't a dry bite?

There is an **antivenom** available! Yay!

No antivenom? Then:

You will begin to tingle near the bite area. That will be followed by a numb feeling.

You will get nauseous . . .

... and a headache and generally feel pretty awful.

> **Antivenom:** a special type of medicine doctors can inject to help treat extra-venomous bites and stings.

And if you are very young, like, baby young . . .

You may get muscle spasms, your heart rate may skyrocket, and you could fall unconscious.

NO, THANK YOU, MOUSIE. AND STAY AWAY FROM THE BABIES, PLEASE! BUT ARE YOU THE DEADLIEST?

Like their mouse spider neighbors, funnel-web spiders make underground homes.

Their front doors feature spangles of silk spreading in every direction.

Party in the front!

The silk works as an alarm system.

Don't need a doorbell camera!

If a tasty meal like an earthworm or a cricket trips over a front door string, BOOM!

Out comes the spider, in goes the meal.

WHAT HAPPENS IF A FUNNEL-WEB SPIDER BITES YOU?

Good news! Funnel-web spider antivenom exists!
So you probably won't die!

But what if you can't get to the hospital in time?

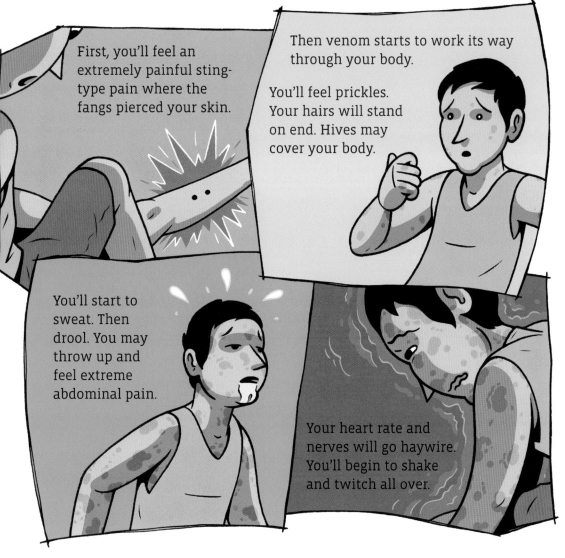

First, you'll feel an extremely painful sting-type pain where the fangs pierced your skin.

Then venom starts to work its way through your body.

You'll feel prickles. Your hairs will stand on end. Hives may cover your body.

You'll start to sweat. Then drool. You may throw up and feel extreme abdominal pain.

Your heart rate and nerves will go haywire. You'll begin to shake and twitch all over.

It may become difficult to breathe, which will affect your brain and further harm your already overtaxed heart.

Over the next hour and a half to several hours, your body will violently shut down.

WHAT DID WE SAY ABOUT SHAKING SHOES? THIS SOUNDS TERRIBLE!
BUT IS IT THE MOST TERRIBLE? LET'S FIND OUT WHO'S NEXT!

Deserts may lack trees and steady rivers, but they still hold plenty of life.

Including six-eyed sand spiders.

They look like miniature crabs covered in little tufts of fur.

The fur catches sand, which the spider hurls on its back . . .

. . . which makes it almost invisible in the desert landscape.

Then it waits.

And it waits.

What is it waiting for?

No, not you! It's waiting for food!

It pounces on unlucky scorpions, insects, and spiders that cross its path.
Then it sinks in its fangs, paralyzing its meal with the toxic venom.

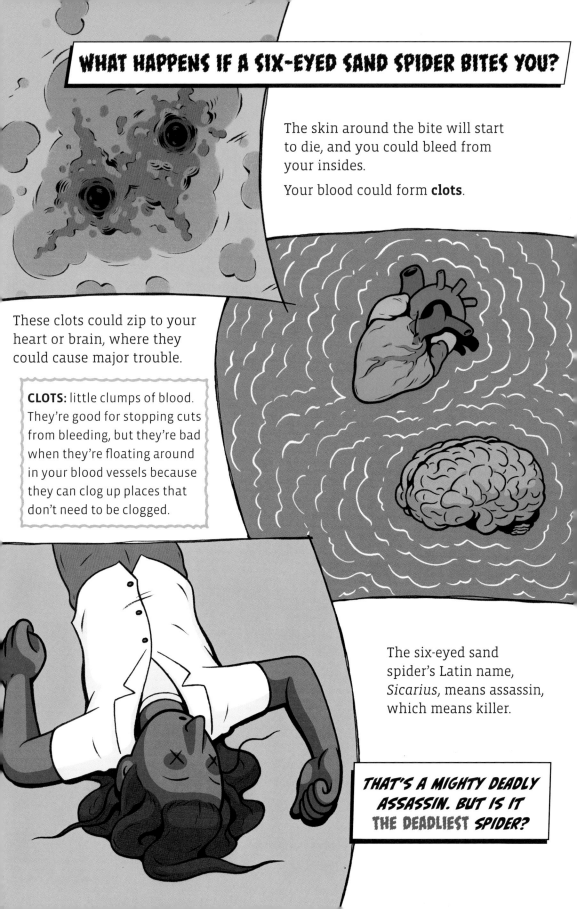

WHAT HAPPENS IF A SIX-EYED SAND SPIDER BITES YOU?

The skin around the bite will start to die, and you could bleed from your insides.

Your blood could form **clots**.

These clots could zip to your heart or brain, where they could cause major trouble.

> **CLOTS:** little clumps of blood. They're good for stopping cuts from bleeding, but they're bad when they're floating around in your blood vessels because they can clog up places that don't need to be clogged.

The six-eyed sand spider's Latin name, *Sicarius*, means assassin, which means killer.

THAT'S A MIGHTY DEADLY ASSASSIN. BUT IS IT THE DEADLIEST SPIDER?

BRAZILIAN WANDERING SPIDER

Number of people bitten each year: thousands

Distribution: Costa Rica and eastern parts of South America

They come out at night.

They roam the forests of South and Central America, hunting small **vertebrates**.

VERTEBRATE: an animal with a backbone.

Brazilian wandering spiders are so large they could easily cover a grown-up's hand.

Or your face.

GAAAAAAAAAAAAAH!

Do YOU have a backbone? OH NO! WATCH OUT FOR BRAZILIAN WANDERING SPIDERS!

Just kidding. You're way too big for one of these creatures to want to eat you. It would be like if you tried to eat a bowl of ice cream the size of a skyscraper. It *sounds* nice but it wouldn't really work that well.

They don't want to cover your face. They want you to go away so they can do spider things.

If you bother one, they'll try to tell you to go away the only way they know how.

They'll lean back on their back legs and wave their front legs in the air.

They'll show you their fangs.

This is spider language for RUN AWAY! WHY DON'T YOU JUST RUN AWAY???

WHAT HAPPENS IF A BRAZILIAN WANDERING SPIDER BITES YOU?

First, it'll hurt. A lot.

Your body will swell around the bite.

You'll start to sweat, get agitated, and feel nauseous.

Then you'll start to throw up and drool, and tears will pour from your eyes even if you're not crying. (You probably will be crying.)

It can get worse.

You will shake as your muscles cramp and shudder.

You will begin to breathe uncontrollably fast as your heart races.

Eventually your nervous system could go into shock. You will be unable to control your blood pressure or body temperature.

Your lips and fingernails could turn blue as you weave in and out of consciousness.

BUT WILL YOU DIE? THIS IS A BOOK ABOUT THE DEADLIEST! AND IT'S TIME TO FIND OUT WHO THAT REALLY IS.

METER

AUSTRALIAN FUNNEL-WEB SPIDER
Average number of people confirmed killed each year: zero
But! 11 people died in the 53 years before an antivenom was developed.

SIX-EYED SAND SPIDER
Average number of people confirmed killed each year: zero

BRAZILIAN WANDERING SPIDER
Average number of people confirmed killed each year: zero
But! There have been two confirmed deaths since 1903.

WHO IS THE DEADLIEST SPIDER?

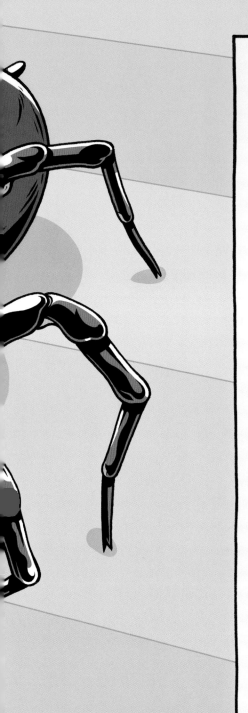

This arachnid has killed more people than the other spiders.

But is it really deadly?

Since antivenom was developed for our deadliest spider, zero people have died from its bite.

Each year . . .

. . . at least 23 people die from playing video games.

Zero people die from widow spider bites.

. . . 2,000 people die from being struck by lightning.

Zero people die from brown recluse bites.

. . . 2,500 left-handed people die from using right-handed tools.

Zero people die from mouse spider bites.

. . . 60,000 people die from rabies.

Zero people die from Australian funnel-web spider bites.

. . . 640,000 people die from falling.

Zero people die from six-eyed sand spider bites.

. . . 7 million people die from air pollution.

Less than one person dies from Brazilian wandering spider bites.

They might hurt, but spider bites very rarely kill anyone.

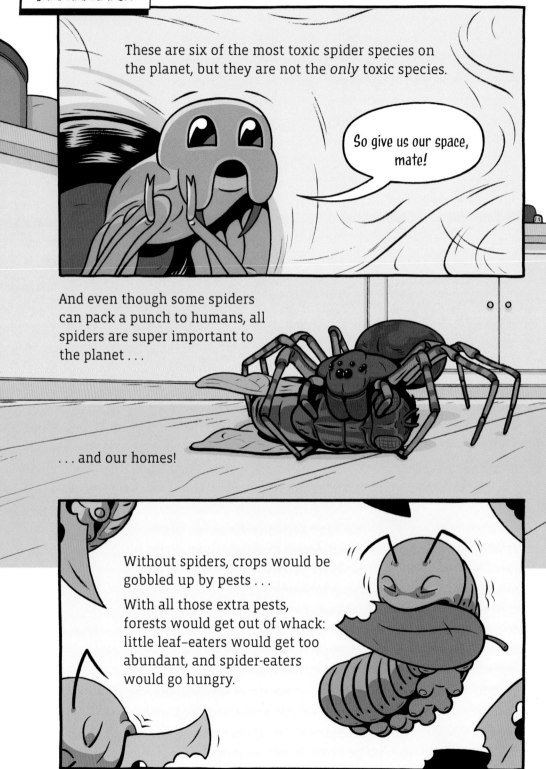

These are six of the most toxic spider species on the planet, but they are not the *only* toxic species.

So give us our space, mate!

And even though some spiders can pack a punch to humans, all spiders are super important to the planet . . .

. . . and our homes!

Without spiders, crops would be gobbled up by pests . . .

With all those extra pests, forests would get out of whack: little leaf–eaters would get too abundant, and spider-eaters would go hungry.

Spiders are among the first creatures to show up after a disaster, like a forest fire or flood, serving as food for those who come next and restoring the soil with their nutritious poops. Without them our planet would have a much harder time recovering from disasters.

Today we even use toxic spider venom to help treat human problems, from upset tummies to weird infections.

ULTIMATE DEADLY!

Each of these deadly spiders has its own superpower. Combine them to create your own Ultimate Deadly creature! Use these superpowers, or discover more and use those!

SIX-EYED SAND SPIDER

Superpower:

Camouflage expert

AUSTRALIAN FUNNEL-WEB SPIDER

Superpower:

Tunnel house

BRAZILIAN WANDERING SPIDER

Superpower:

Wicked warning pose

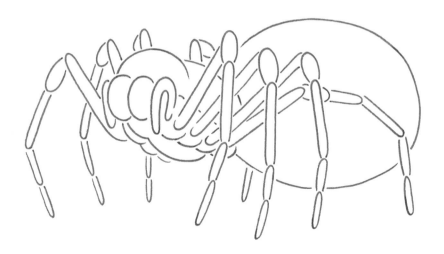

MOUSE SPIDER

Superpower:

Extra-powerful fangs

BROWN RECLUSE SPIDER

Superpower:

Secretive and shy

BLACK WIDOW SPIDER

Superpower:

Hourglass warning